ODYSSEUS, SUPERHERO

ABOUT THE AUTHORS

Tony Robinson plays Baldrick in the television series, <u>Black Adder</u> and presents and co-produces Channel 4's archaeology series, <u>Time Team</u>. He wrote four series of BBC TV's <u>Maid Marian and Her Merry Men</u> in which he also played the Sheriff of Nottingham. He has written sixteen children's books and has won numerous awards as a writer of children's television programmes, including two Royal Television Society awards, a BAFTA, and the International Prix Jeunesse. He has appeared in over one thousand television programmes but enjoys staying in his Bristol home, writing.

Richard Curtis began writing comedy after leaving Oxford University in 1978. He has written for, amongst others, <u>Not the Nine O'Clock News</u>, <u>Black Adder</u>, <u>Mr Bean</u>, <u>The Vicar of Dibley</u>, and <u>Comic Relief</u>, which he co-founded and co-produces for the BBC. He has also written two films, <u>The Tall Guy</u> and <u>Four Weddings And A Funeral</u>, for which he won the Writers Guild Awards in America and the UK and the Evening Standard, Comedy and London Critics Awards. In order to prepare for this book he studied Classics at Papplewick and Harrow School, and Greek at Oxford. He was made an MBE in 1994, and lives in Notting Hill with his partner, Emma Freud, and their daughter, Scarlett.

Odysseus, Superhero

Tony Robinson and Richard Curtis

Illustrated by Chris Smedley

Hodder
Children's
Books

a division of Hodder Headline plc

Text copyright © Tony Robinson and Richard Curtis 1986
Illustrations copyright © Chris Smedley 1996

First published in Great Britain in 1986
by the British Broadcasting Corporation/Knight Books

This edition published 1996 by Hodder Children's Books

This book is based on the BBC TV series *Odysseus – The Greatest Hero
of Them All* by Tony Robinson and Richard Curtis, told by Tony
Robinson, produced by Angela Beeching and directed by David Bell.

The right of Tony Robinson and Richard Curtis to be identified as the
Authors of the Work has been asserted by them in accordance with the
Copyright, Designs and Patents Act 1988.

10 9 8 7 6 5 4

A Catalogue record for this book is available from the British Library

ISBN 0 340 66497 5

Typeset by Phoenix Typesetting, Ilkley, West Yorkshire

Printed and bound in Great Britain by
Cox & Wyman Ltd, Reading, Berks.

Hodder Children's Books
a division of Hodder Headline plc
338 Euston Road
London NW1 3BH

*Also available from Hodder Children's Books
by Tony Robinson and Richard Curtis*

Odysseus Goes Through Hell
Theseus, Monster-killer

1
The Golden Slag Heap

Deep in the bushes the tiny puppy stood completely still. Occasionally, its eyes flicked up to the boy crouched beside it. He was sixteen, short, with dark hair. In one hand he held a rope and in the other a spear.

Suddenly the puppy's ears pricked up. The moment he and the boy had been waiting for had arrived. First there was a crashing sound, then a snorting sound, then a thundering sound, and suddenly a huge wild boar crashed, snorted and thundered out of the forest, coming straight at them. At first neither of them could believe how huge it was, and how fast it was running. The boar charged at them, its huge tusks shining, closer and closer, twenty metres, ten metres, only one metre away. In two seconds they'd both be dead, but neither moved. And then, fast as lightning, the boy tugged on the rope and –

WHOOSH – the boar shot up into the air, and – SQUEAL – hung in mid-air, struggling and kicking, trapped in the boy's net.

'It worked!' he shouted, and rushed forwards, his eyes shining.

But it hadn't worked. Because at that very moment, the rope snapped, and the huge animal crashed to the ground. The boy tried to run but there was no time. Wild with fury, the boar shook itself free of the net and charged. On the first charge it almost got him, but he dived out of the way just in time. The second time he wasn't so lucky. The boy swerved, but the boar swerved too, and the boy felt a dreadful, searing pain as the huge white tusk cut deep into his leg. He yelled, the puppy squealed, the boar snorted in triumph and then – BANG – everything went black.

The next thing the boy was aware of was the sound of two voices above him. He looked up, and saw two old men peering down.

'My goodness,' one of them said. 'Look who it is!'

'Yes,' said the other, 'it certainly is. It's Odysseus, the King's son.'

And they were right. Lying there on the ground, blood pouring from his leg, was Odysseus, the King's son – the boy who would grow up into one of the greatest heroes ever known. But there was nothing heroic about him now. He took one look at his leg, and the red pool of blood, and passed out again.

When he woke, he thought he was dead and had gone to hell. All around him there were flames and chanting and drums. Dancers with huge painted masks whirled round him, screeching, yelling, and then rushing up to him and pouring oil on his wounded leg. Then suddenly one dancer broke away from the others. He was more frightening than the rest. He had an enormous red mask with a mad grinning mouth, which peered down into Odysseus' face with wild staring eyes. If he wasn't dead already, Odysseus was sure he was about to die.

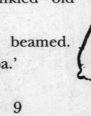

In a last wild gesture, he tore at the horrible mask to see the horrible face that must lie beneath it. But it wasn't a horrible face at all. In fact, there behind the hideous red mask was . . . the smiling face of a rather pleasant, wrinkled old gentleman.

'Hallo sunshine,' he beamed. 'Say hallo to your grandpa.'

'Grandfather!' said Odysseus in amazement. 'I thought you'd died years ago.'

'No,' laughed the wizened old man. 'They threw me out of court and pretended I was dead.'

'Why would they do that?' asked Odysseus.

'Because I was always telling lies and nicking things.'

'Oh dear,' said Odysseus.

'Not quite what you'd expect of a member of the Royal Family, eh?' said his grandfather, and then burst out laughing again.

'It certainly isn't,' agreed Odysseus, but couldn't resist smiling himself. He was rather getting to like the sound of the old man's voice.

'You see,' said his grandpa, 'I wouldn't be too sure it's always good to be *too* good. When the going gets tough, it's not a bad idea to be a little crafty once in a while, do a little nicking here, tell the odd fib there.' He paused, 'For instance, will you be in trouble when you get home?'

'Not half,' said Odysseus. 'I'm not supposed to go boar hunting alone. I'll be in so much trouble I'll wish I'd never been born.'

'Then tell them you fell down a mine shaft and hurt your leg.'

'But that would be lying!' said Odysseus.

'Exactly,' said his grandpa, and let out the loudest laugh yet.

'Where have you been?' roared Odysseus' father, the

King, when his son got back to the palace.

'I fell down a mine shaft,' said Odysseus.

'Oh, well, fair enough,' said his dad. 'I thought you might have gone off boar hunting again, and then there would have been trouble.'

'Oh, no, I'd never do that,' said Odysseus quickly, and you could have sworn that a little grin, just like his grandfather's, spread over his face.

'Good,' said his father. He was sitting on a large, bronze throne at the end of a huge, crumbling hall: the grandest hall in the dilapidated palace. Beside him sat the Queen, who was very worried about Odysseus' leg, now that she knew it hadn't been caused by him boar hunting on his own.

'Then take a look at this. Tell me what you make of it.' He handed Odysseus a golden scroll with grand silver and gold lettering on it.

Odysseus read it through carefully. It said:

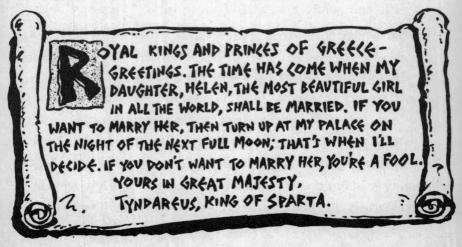

ROYAL KINGS AND PRINCES OF GREECE – GREETINGS. THE TIME HAS COME WHEN MY DAUGHTER, HELEN, THE MOST BEAUTIFUL GIRL IN ALL THE WORLD, SHALL BE MARRIED. IF YOU WANT TO MARRY HER, THEN TURN UP AT MY PALACE ON THE NIGHT OF THE NEXT FULL MOON; THAT'S WHEN I'LL DECIDE. IF YOU DON'T WANT TO MARRY HER, YOU'RE A FOOL.
YOURS IN GREAT MAJESTY,
TYNDAREUS, KING OF SPARTA.

And then, over the page, there was an extra bit:

P.S. Bring a present.

Odysseus' mother was very excited. Sparta was one of the greatest Kingdoms in the land, and Tyndareus a great and powerful King. 'Imagine the glory,' she chirped, 'if you married Helen. You wouldn't just be King of this tiny island. You'd be King of Sparta as well.'

'Yes,' said Odysseus, without much enthusiasm. He was very fond of the tiny island of Ithaca, and very happy to be King of it and nowhere else; least of all Sparta, where he'd heard that people took things rather seriously and never told jokes.

'What about the present?' he asked.

'Take this leather purse,' said his father. 'It holds twenty gold pieces – it's all we can afford. Give them to Tyndareus and bring us back a daughter-in-law.'

'I'll see what I can do,' mumbled Odysseus, and limped out of the chamber, his leg still hurting badly.

Back in his room, his old nurse tended to the wound.

'It's going to leave an awful scar,' she fussed.

'I wouldn't worry,' said Odysseus. 'Means you'll be able to recognise me if I ever get my head cut off.'

'Oh, you bad boy,' she scolded, but they both had a good laugh. And Odysseus thought . . . *mm, I wonder how many good laughs I'd get married to the most beautiful woman in the world. I'm not sure about the idea – got a feeling she might*

be trouble. Still . . . and he bounced the twenty gold pieces in his hands, and winced a bit as the bandage went on.

Five days later, Odysseus found himself at the palace of King Tyndareus. The moon was full, and the court-yard was absolutely full as well. Everywhere there were Princes.

You have never seen so many Princes in one place. There were tall ones, short ones, medium-sized ones. There was one with a fat belly and a spotty nose, one with a thin belly and a spotty nose, and one very large one with a perfectly nice nose, but gigantic, sticking-out ears. And right at the front stood an enormous bearded one with a leopard skin over his head and shoulders, towering over all the rest.

Not that they were behaving as you would think Princes should. They were pushing and shoving each other left and right, all trying to get closer to the front to catch a glimpse of Helen. She was after all the most beautiful girl in the world, and they had all come in the hope of marrying her. But so far, she hadn't put in an appearance, and tempers were getting short.

Then suddenly a trumpet sounded, and a voice announced: 'Silence. Helen will now take the evening air.'

And there was silence. And everyone waited. And then, high on the battlements above them, a little door opened and the Princes gasped with wonder.

Out, into the moonlight, stepped Helen. On top of the palace wall she strolled by the light of the moon, a veil hanging elegantly over her face, and a train hanging behind her, held by a rather sweet-looking, perky girl.

It was a beautiful sight, and for a moment, the evening was still and silent. Only for a moment though, for suddenly all the Princes started pushing forward to get a better look, and trouble started. Someone fell, and then someone else fell on top of him, and the one who fell punched the one who'd pushed him and soon there was a full fight going on.

Odysseus, cunning as ever, took care to avoid it. He was so short he hadn't seen a thing when Helen first came out, so now he wriggled his way forward, past punches and between legs, until only one thing was blocking his view. Or rather two things. The two gigantic ears of the gigantic Prince.

15

'Excuse me,' said Odysseus, tapping him on the shoulder. 'What was your name again?'

'Prince Ajax,' replied the giant Prince. 'Why?'

'Well, there's someone at the back wants a word with you; says it's important.'

'Oh, fine,' said Big Ajax and, as he disappeared, Odysseus took his place, and looked up to where Helen was.

'Is that all there is to see?' he complained. 'Some girl with a cloth over her head? How do I know if I fancy her or not? She might have two noses and three eyes, for all I know.'

'She'd still be better looking than you,' said a voice from above him. It was the perky girl carrying Helen's train, and she was smiling straight at him. Odysseus liked the look of her, and was just about to smile back when, VUMP, a terrific blow smacked on the back of his head and he smashed to the ground. Above him hovered a huge fist. It was the fist of Big Ajax and he was not looking happy.

'You little liar,' he thundered. 'No one wanted to see me.'

'Didn't they?' said Odysseus innocently and tried to pull off the helmet which was now jammed right down over his eyes. It wasn't an easy job and it didn't help that someone seemed to be laughing at him. When at last he did pull it off, he saw who it was. Disappearing through the door at the end of the battlements was the girl with the train, just laughing and laughing and laughing.

That evening, Odysseus was sitting in the courtyard when high above his head he heard the girl's laugh

again. It came from a room three floors up, with a tiny window, and Odysseus thought, *mm, why not take a look?*

So he grabbed some ivy, climbed up and very cautiously peered through the window. Inside were two girls. The one facing him was the laughing girl from the battlements. She was combing the hair of another girl he could hardly see. But then suddenly she turned and Odysseus froze. He knew at once who it was: she was thirteen or fourteen and she was incredibly beautiful. It was Helen.

'Give me a sweet, Penelope,' she said.
But Penelope, laughing as ever,
grabbed a huge box of chocolates
and hid them behind her back.

'If you have any more of these,'
she said, 'you'll be Helen the fat,
not Helen the beautiful.'

'Nonsense. I'm sure if I were fat,
I'd still be beautiful,' replied Helen, and snatched the chocolates back. 'Let's see . . .'

'Which one are you going to choose?' asked Penelope.

'The orange cream or the hazelnut cluster, I think,' replied Helen thoughtfully.

'No, silly billy. Which Prince?'

'Oh, that,' said Helen, taking the orange cream *and* the hazelnut cluster. 'The richest, I suppose – I'm not bothered really. I mean, they're all stupid, aren't they?

Did you see that silly little one with the helmet jammed over his face?'

They both laughed, remembering Odysseus. Fortunately for him though, they were spluttering so much with giggles that he couldn't make out exactly what they were saying. He peered in even closer, when suddenly Penelope looked up, and seemed to stare straight at him. Quickly he ducked down below the window sill. Had she seen him? He thought not.

A few seconds later he summoned up the courage to peer over the window sill again, and saw Penelope turn away, walk over to the bed, take something from underneath it and stride back towards the window. He ducked again, quickly.

'What's the matter?' asked Helen. 'Is there someone at the window?'

'No,' said Penelope. 'I'm just emptying the chamber pot.' And, without a second's warning, she flung the contents out of the window, right on top of Odysseus' head.

'Mind you,' she said, turning back into the room, 'if there had been someone at the window, it would have served him right for snooping, wouldn't it? Now, let's have another laugh about that Prince with the helmet jammed over his eyes . . .'

But by that time, Odysseus had lost interest in the conversation. He needed a wash, because he was covered in something, and it wasn't rose-water.

Next morning was the morning of the great decision.

The Princes were all spruce and tidy and lined up to give their presents to Helen's father.

At the front was Menelaus, the richest man in Greece. He was hairy and huge and ugly but, boy, was he rich!

At the back was Odysseus, the poorest Prince of the lot, with his twenty pieces of gold.

The trumpet sounded and Menelaus stepped forward. 'Tyndareus, King of Sparta,' he announced, 'I humbly offer you a thousand gold pieces, twenty chests of silver, and five hundred gold goblets.'

CRASH! Menelaus' slaves dropped them on the floor in front of the King.

GULP! Odysseus knew he didn't stand much chance. *What a waste of twenty gold pieces,* he thought, fingering his purse.

Next came Menelaus' brother, Agamemnon, the finest soldier in Greece. He was the huge one in the leopard skin, and there were diamonds where the eyes of the leopard should have been.

'I present fifty suits of armour, two hundred helmets, and a thousand assorted daggers,' he called out.

CRASH! they went on the pile.

GULP! Odysseus knew he had no chance at all, and

he slipped all but a handful of the gold pieces back into his pocket. No point wasting it.

And so on, one after another, the Princes added their gifts until there was a huge gold slag heap in front of King Tyndareus.

At last it was Odysseus' turn. He stepped forward bravely. 'I'm the Crown Prince of the island kingdom of Ithaca. I humbly offer you, ahm, three gold pieces,' he announced, and waited for the laughter.

But no one was listening, because just at that moment, a fight started. Big Ajax grabbed one of the spotty-nosed Princes and was banging his head against the wall.

'Listen, Spotty,' he was saying, 'don't tell me I won't get her. I haven't come all this way for nothing. I'm going to marry Helen, and that's that.'

'Rubbish!' shouted Agamemnon, 'I am!' and sent Ajax crashing to the floor.

'No, I am!' yelled everyone else, and whoopsidaisy, suddenly they were all fighting again. Odysseus ducked as tables went crashing and bodies went flying. It was all quite good natured, until suddenly there was a glint of bronze as a dagger was drawn.

In a flash, Odysseus sprinted to the top of the treasure and yelled, 'Stop!'

And – amazingly – everyone did. In mid punch. They all turned and stared at the small chap on top of the gold pile.

'What is it?' asked Menelaus.

'One of the eyes has dropped out of Agamemnon's leopard,' replied Odysseus.

'Oh no,' moaned Agamemnon. 'That's my best leopard.'

'I know,' said Odysseus. 'We've all got our best clothes on and they'll be ruined if we're not careful.'

'Good point,' agreed Agamemnon.

'Also, just by the way, someone might get killed,' added Odysseus. 'So, let's take a vow.'

'What vow?'

'Let's take a vow that Helen can marry whoever she wants to, and that no one will try to take her away from him, and . . . if anyone does ever try, let's swear that all of us will join together and get her back.'

'Good idea,' said Agamemnon. Everyone agreed. Even Big Ajax.

And so it was that two minutes later they were all standing in a circle in the middle of the room; the most powerful men in the world all together. Drawing their daggers, they cut their right hands, and, as the blood dripped on to the pile of gold, they swore Odysseus' vow: Helen could marry whom she liked, and the Princes would always defend them both. There was silence, broken only by the drip of red blood on gold.

Suddenly a girl's voice spoke out behind them. 'I've made my choice.' The Princes all turned. There stood Helen, dressed in a short white dress with daisies in her hair. She looked beautiful, and each one knew at that moment that he wished she'd choose him. This was a woman worth fighting for.

'And the man I've chosen is . . . ahm . . .'

'Menelaus,' whispered Penelope.

'That's right. Menelaus,' said Helen.

Menelaus' eyes flashed in triumph, and for a moment none of the other Princes could believe what they'd heard. But the decision was made and that was that. Slowly they turned and left the room. Menelaus had won.

The moment they were gone, King Tyndareus breathed a sigh of relief. He had thought that his palace was going to be smashed to pieces, but apart from the odd broken pot, it was still intact. He turned to Odysseus, who was hanging around in the corner picking up the odd piece of treasure that had been scattered in the fight.

'Odysseus, Prince of Ithaca, how can I ever repay you for stopping that brawl?'

'Well,' said Odysseus, with a grin playing on his face. 'I came for a wife, and I don't want to leave without one.'

'Any idea who you'd like?' said Tyndareus.

And Odysseus looked up at the laughing girl who had emptied the chamber pot over him, and smiled another big broad grin. 'Well, as a matter of fact, I have.'

Half an hour later, Odysseus was driving his chariot back to Ithaca with Penelope by his side. 'It's a small island,' he was saying. 'It's not rich, but you'll love it. And I'll introduce you to my grandfather, who's a real rogue. And if it's not quite posh enough, I'll build you a new palace. And in a year and a half, when I'm eighteen, my father's going to abdicate, so I'll be King. What do you think?'

But Penelope didn't say a thing.

'Look, please say something,' he pleaded. 'You haven't opened your mouth since we left Sparta.'

'Why should I?' snapped Penelope. 'You've taken me from my home, I don't know you, I don't know your island and why on earth should I want to meet your grandfather? What do you expect me to say?'

Odysseus slammed on the chariot brakes. 'Look,' he said, 'there are seventeen gold coins here in my pocket. Take them if you like, and make your way home. If you don't want to come, you don't have to.'

Penelope paused, looked at him, then took the money, stepped out of the chariot and began to walk politely home. Odysseus cracked his whip and the chariot roared off in the other direction. He wasn't going to beg.

Five minutes later, the chariot was back and Odysseus jumped out. 'Please,' he begged, 'I would like, more than anything in the world, for you to come to Ithaca and be the Queen. Come on. How about it?'

There was a pause. 'If I can drive the chariot,' said Penelope, and let out a raucous laugh.

'What are you laughing at?' asked Odysseus.

'Well,' giggled Penelope, 'don't think you're ever getting your gold coins back, loverboy.'

And with that she leapt into the chariot, snatched the reins and they both shot off towards Ithaca. Ahead of them lay a beautiful pink and orange sunset. But at their backs, the black clouds of night were already gathering.

2
The Burly Nun

It was a year later. Odysseus was King and Penelope had decided that she liked everything about Ithaca, except the old palace, because bits of plaster kept falling on her head.

'I thought you said we were going to get a new palace,' said Penelope.

'That's right,' agreed Odysseus. 'Where shall we build it?'

'Just here,' said Penelope, standing on a little round hill overlooking the city.

'But there's an enormous old olive tree in the way. I don't want that chopped down.'

'Then we'll leave it where it is,' retorted Penelope. 'We'll build the only palace in the world with an enormous tree sticking through the roof.'

And they did. The new palace was the most magnificent building on the island. It had a huge throne room with a large bronze throne, and right through the middle of the royal bedroom grew a massive tree trunk.

'Don't you think it'll get in the way?' asked Odysseus doubtfully.

'No,' replied Penelope, 'I've got an idea . . .'

And together they carved a huge double bed out of the tree trunk and, in summer, olives dangled over their heads while they slept. They were young and their lives stretched before them.

One morning Odysseus was lying in bed, thinking about the day ahead. Before lunch he would go and put some flowers on the grave of his grandfather; in the afternoon he would visit his parents at their retirement cottage in the hills; and this evening he and Penelope would sit in the Great Hall and plan how to make Ithaca great and happy.

There was a gurgling sound from the other side of the room. Odysseus spat out an olive stone and looked across to where the nurse was rocking his baby son and heir Telemachus to sleep.

Little did he know that after tomorrow he wouldn't see his son again, until the child had grown up.

Suddenly he heard a commotion outside. 'Where's Odysseus?' someone was shouting. 'They're coming to get him.'

Odysseus raced along the high street to the docks. A boat had landed from the mainland and pouring down the gangplank were holiday makers and merchants and foreign tourists and parties of school children, and in the middle of them all, surrounded by pigs, was the old pig man Eumaeus. When he saw Odysseus, Eumaeus elbowed his way through the throng.

'Menelaus is coming,' he said in a hoarse whisper.

'And he's bringing his whole army. There's going to be a war – and he says you've got to fight. Some idiot made all the Greek kings and princes swear they'd get his wife back if she was ever stolen – and she has been!'

Oh dear, thought Odysseus, *it seemed like a good idea at the time. What do I do now? I don't want to go to war.*

And then he remembered what his grandfather had said. 'When the going gets tough, it's not a bad idea to be a bit crafty.' And a crafty grin spread over his face.

A week later Menelaus' golden boat arrived at Ithaca. It was so big it filled the entire harbour. Soldiers and noblemen streamed off and marched up the high street in their emerald green armour. Menelaus walked at the front, with sweat trickling down from his golden crown, and at his right shoulder was a man with a silver bow and a quiver full of silver arrows. At first it looked as though he was squinting, but if you peered closer you could see that one eye was missing. The other was the one he aimed with. He was Philoctetes, a very cunning man and the finest archer in the world.

Menelaus turned to him. 'Philoctetes,' he said, 'go and find Odysseus.'

The high street was deserted except for an old man asleep in a chair surrounded by piglets. Philoctetes kicked the chair over and the piglets ran off squealing. Then, quick as lightning, Philoctetes drew his bow and an arrow was pointing at the old man's throat. 'Pigman,' he snapped. 'Where's your King?'

'He's up there ploughing,' said Eumaeus pointing to the top of the cliff. 'But I don't think you'll like what you're going to see.'

And he was right. Half an hour later Menelaus' soldiers had reached the top of the path. And what they

saw amazed them. Instead of a normal field, ploughed in straight lines, the ground was a mass of wild and wavey shapes, triangles and circles. And there, on top of the plough, was a strange sight – a man dressed in rags with a crown on his head and a mad stare in his eyes. And between his plough shafts were a sheep and a donkey in a straw hat.

'Gee up,' said the mad man, and the animals lumbered forward.

'That's Odysseus,' explained the pig man.

'What does he think he's doing?' asked Menelaus.

'Plough the field. Plough the field. Plough the field,' jibbered Odysseus.

'He's mad,' said Eumaeus, but Odysseus took no notice. He started to throw something into the crazy furrows.

'Sow the seed. Sow the seed. Sow the seed,' he chanted. But it wasn't seed. It was biscuit crumbs.

'He's stark staring bonkers,' said Menelaus. 'I don't want men like that in my army. Come on, lads. Back to the mainland.'

'He's either very mad or very cunning,' murmured Philoctetes, his one eye flashing. 'Let's put him to the test. Pigman, does he have any children?'

'Just one – a baby son,' answered Eumaeus, and immediately wished he hadn't.

Philoctetes sprinted to the palace, burst into the bedroom, snatched Telemachus from the nurse's arms and then raced back. He pushed his way through the crowd, laid the baby in front of the plough and stepped back to watch. Nearer and nearer came the plough, its huge blades flashing.

'Let's see how mad he really is,' said Philoctetes with a leer, as the plough sliced through the grass throwing up huge clods of earth and showering the soldiers. Meanwhile little Telemachus just lay there gurgling.

Now the plough was really close, but Odysseus' mad eyes stared straight ahead. He didn't seem to notice that he was about to chop his baby son into little pieces. Eumaeus shut his eyes in horror . . .

'Whoa,' shouted Odysseus, and the plough came to a

33

halt so close to Telemachus that the sheep bent down and licked the baby's face.

'Odysseus isn't mad,' crowed Philoctetes triumphantly.

'No, I'm not mad,' replied Odysseus. 'I'm *furious*. You could have killed my son,' and he picked the baby up and hugged him tenderly.

'Odysseus,' called out Menelaus. 'Do you remember the day you persuaded the Princes of Greece to swear that if my wife Helen was stolen they'd help to get her back?'

How can I ever forget, thought Odysseus. 'Err, vaguely,' he replied.

'Well, she's been taken away by Paris, the youngest son of the King of Troy. Will you honour your vow?'

Odysseus looked at Menelaus, all hairy and ferocious, and he looked at the army of hairy and ferocious men behind him, and he knew what his answer had to be.

Next morning, down at the quayside, Odysseus held his baby son tightly and kissed his wife goodbye.

'Don't worry,' he said, 'I'll be back very soon.' But his brow darkened. He knew life was not always as easy as it seemed.

'I'll wait for you,' said Penelope.

'Don't wait forever,' came the reply. 'You know what can happen in a war. If I'm not back by the time Telemachus is a man, promise me you'll marry again.'

'I promise,' answered Penelope, hugging her husband tightly. She knew as she held him how much she loved him.

Slowly Menelaus' huge boat pulled away from the harbour and behind it ten smaller boats set off, each one containing a hundred men of Ithaca. Penelope waved until they disappeared over the horizon.

When the Ithacan fleet arrived at the Greek port of Aulis it was already jam-packed with boats. No one could get in or out. Sailors were arguing; boats were tangled up in each other's rigging; and in the centre of it all was General Agamemnon, Menelaus' brother, leaping from boat to boat, shouting instructions, patting people on the back, knocking others into the sea. And on the quay-side was Calchas, the old archbishop, with a white pointed beard and a huge silver coat covered in stars. He was yelling at Agamemnon.

'How many times have I told you there's no point in invading Troy till we're properly prepared. You haven't made one single sacrifice yet.'

'Leave me alone,' shouted Agamemnon.

'And where's Achilles? The fleet can't go without him. He's the strongest, bravest man in Greece. He can wrestle with lions, he can squash elephants. I even saw him kill a hippopotamus with his little finger.'

'I'm afraid he won't be coming,' replied Agamemnon. 'His mother doesn't want him to fight and she's hidden him so well that even my most brilliant spies haven't been able to find him.'

'I've heard he's staked out on the island of Scyros,' said Diomedes, the Prince with a big spotty nose and a belly hanging over his trousers. 'I'll go and take a look if you like.'

'Send Odysseus with him,' said Menelaus. 'He's the craftiest Greek I've ever met. If anyone can find Achilles, he can.'

'But he's a cheat,' protested Philoctetes.

'And a liar,' shrieked big Ajax.

'Sounds like just the man for the job,' said Diomedes smiling. 'I'll take him.'

Odysseus and Diomedes searched every single nook and cranny on Scyros but everywhere they drew a complete blank.

'There's only one place left to look,' said Diomedes, 'and that's the nunnery. But if he's in there, how on earth are we going to winkle him out?'

'I've got a plan,' said Odysseus.

'I thought you might,' replied Diomedes.

An hour later Odysseus was knocking on the nunnery door disguised as a travelling salesman.

'Roll up, roll up!' he shouted. 'Mirrors, manicure sets, holy relics, all at bargain prices.'

Hordes of excited nuns dragged him into the nunnery and slammed the door behind him.

So far so good, he thought and tipped the contents of his sack on the ground. 'Scissors,' he shouted, 'winter vests, a great big sword, boiled sweets. Buy now while stocks last.'

The nuns clustered round him. Short nuns, fat nuns, skinny nuns, one extremely tall nun. They peered into the mirrors, tasted the sweets, held up the vests to see if they fitted, when suddenly there was a terrifying hammering at the door and Diomedes' voice boomed out, 'Yo, ho, ho, I'm the pirate king and I'm going to burn down the nunnery and sell you all as slaves.'

The nuns were extremely sensible. They didn't panic. They didn't scream. Some started to bar the door, some began to hide, others grabbed scissors to protect themselves. But the extremely tall nun behaved in an extremely un-nunlike fashion. She tucked her dress up into her knickers, rolled up her sleeves to reveal a massive pair of hairy arms, grabbed a great big sword and started swinging it round and round her head.

'Excuse me,' said Odysseus. 'Don't I know you?'

'Please don't interrupt me,' replied the nun. 'I'm about to decapitate a pirate king.'

'You're Achilles, aren't you?' insisted Odysseus.

'Don't put me off,' answered the nun. 'Any minute now this pirate's going to come belting in and . . . hey, wait a minute. How do you know my name?'

'I've come to collect you,' answered Odysseus. 'You've got to go to Troy to fight the Trojans.'

'Have I?' said Achilles sadly. 'Can't I stay here with the girls?'

'No,' replied Odysseus. 'Sorry.' And they sailed back to the mainland.

When they arrived at Aulis the boats were deserted. The whole army was crowded on to the slopes of the hill overlooking the harbour. On the hilltop, in front of a stone altar, stood Calchas, his voice quivering, his arms outstretched and his huge cape billowing in the wind.

'In order to speed the boats to Troy,' he bellowed, 'an

enormous sacrifice has been made and the Gods are grateful. They've brought forth this great wind to carry us on our way. Behold the sacrifice.' He dropped his arms and stepped to one side – and what a sacrifice it was! The Greeks let out a gasp of horror.

On the altar was the body of a young girl – Agamemnon's youngest daughter. And standing by her side was General Agamemnon with a bloody knife in his hand and tears pouring down his face. The whole crowd hushed. There was a silence which seemed to last an age, then – ting! – the knife dropped from Agamemnon's hand and he flung his arms round his daughter and kissed her lifeless body again and again. He'd made the ultimate sacrifice, yet how could he ever forgive himself?

Agamemnon was lost in fear and sorrow, until a sudden cheer roused him. Someone was pushing through to the front, someone the Greeks had been praying would arrive.

'Fear not,' shouted Achilles, 'for I, the people's hero, have returned! Obviously our General is not quite himself at the moment so I will lead you. Who will follow me to burn Troy to the ground?'

'Me! Me! Me!' shouted the men, and raced down the hillside back to their ships. Achilles turned to Odysseus.

'Which way exactly is Troy?' he whispered.

'North-north-east,' replied Odysseus.

'That's what I thought,' called Achilles as he disappeared down the hill after his men.

'Shall we go for the ride?' asked Odysseus.

'I think we better had,' replied Diomedes, scratching his long spotty nose.

Next day the Greek fleet landed near a small seaside town. Achilles leapt off the leading boat and sprinted up the beach.

'Charge!' he yelled.

'Hurrah!' shouted his men and rushed into the town waving their swords in the air.

'Are you sure you know what you're doing?' said Odysseus.

'Have you ever known me to make a mistake?' asked Achilles contemptuously.

Diomedes looked at Odysseus and pulled a face. The

answer was yes – and it looked like he was about to make another one. Within minutes the whole town was ablaze and the market square was littered with bodies.

'Pretty simple operation,' chortled Achilles looking rather pleased with himself.

'But this isn't Troy,' said Diomedes.

'Isn't it?'

'No, it's Mysia,' said Diomedes.

'And the Mysians are on our side,' added Odysseus.

'Oh dear,' said Achilles. 'Cease fire, men!' And he took out a bronze loudspeaker and yelled into it.

'People of Mysia. There appears to have been a slight mix up. Apparently we're all on the same side, but there's no hard feelings and as a gesture of our good faith we are going to throw away our weapons.'

Then he nodded to his men who rather reluctantly dropped their swords and spears. But before the echo of the last weapon had died away there was a roar of anger. The people of Mysia burst out of their blazing buildings and attacked the Greeks with anything they could lay their hands on – pitchforks, logs of wood, razor-sharp scythes. The Greeks turned and fled as best they could. Some were trampled to the ground and beaten; others reached the sea only to be pulled under and drowned.

'Something tells me Agamemnon isn't going to be too happy about this,' murmured Diomedes.

The tattered remnants of the fleet limped back to Aulis. Agamemnon was standing at the quayside, his eyes flashing with fury at the men who had followed Achilles without his blessing. Every tenth man was flogged, and while the sound of the lash still hung in the air, Agamemnon whispered in Achilles' ear, 'Don't you ever try to take my command away from me again.'

Achilles made no reply but from the look on his face you could tell there'd be trouble sooner or later.

Agamemnon stood the rest of the army to attention. Hour after hour they waited for the next order as the sun beat down on them. Finally, towards evening, Agamemnon returned. The eyes of his leopard-skin head-dress flashed in the late afternoon sun as he growled, 'The fun and games are over, lads. It's time to sail to Troy to teach those Trojans a lesson.'

So once more the flotilla sailed out of the harbour. People cheered and waved flags and threw confetti, and bands played the national anthem, and the last thing they heard was Agamemnon shouting back to them, 'Never fear, we'll return covered in glory.'

But Odysseus, standing alone on deck, stared at the dark red sunset staining the sky and muttered, 'Covered in blood, more like.'

3
The Colour of Birds' Eggs

A fiery silver arrow shot from the prow of the leading ship. High in the sky it flew, then down, down, down into the bright green sea. SHHOOOOH!

'That's for King Priam!' shouted Philoctetes, the greatest archer in Greece. 'When the fleet gets to Troy, we'll burn his palace to the ground.'

'HOORAY!' went the sailors. Philoctetes fired again. 'This one's for Hector, Priam's eldest son. He may be the Trojan hero, but our hero Achilles will smash his head to pieces!'

'HOORAY!' went the sailors.

'And this one's for Paris, Priam's youngest son. He stole our Queen Helen, but I'll steal his life away with an arrow deep into his heart!'

By now the sailors were going mad. 'HOORAY!'

Then Philoctetes fired
another burning arrow.
'And this one's for
AAAARGH!'

'Who's Aaaargh?'
asked Big Ajax.

'I shot an arrow through
my foot. Odysseus jogged
me!' screamed Philoctetes.

'Oh dear, I am sorry,' said Odysseus,
who was fed up with Philoctetes
showing off. 'It was an accident.
I tripped over the anchor. Quick –
let me pull out the arrow before
it burns your foot off.'

All that night, Philoctetes lay in his bed moaning. And
all the next day, he kept on moaning.

'When's he going to stop?' asked Big Ajax. 'He's
getting on my nerves, and you know what happens when
something gets on my nerves – things get broken.'

Two days later, the moans were getting worse, and
Ajax had started breaking things.

'Phew, what's that smell?' asked Diomedes.

'It's the foot,' said Odysseus. 'It's going bad.'

'It smells like the inside of a dustbin,' muttered
Menelaus, and he was putting it politely.

In the end it just got too bad to bear. General
Agamemnon lifted his huge, leopard-skin head-dress

and scratched his head.

'Odysseus,' he said,
'do something about
it. That foot's
beginning to attract flies.'

So Odysseus had
a quick think, came up
with a bright idea, and went
on deck. There lay Philoctetes, bluebottles buzzing
round his bright green foot. Odysseus knelt down
beside him, trying not to breathe through his nose.

'See that island over there?' he said.

'Yes,' Philoctetes snapped. 'I'm not blind. What about
it?' Odysseus was not his favourite person.

'Well, it's a pity we're not landing there, that's all. It's
called Limnos and it's jam-packed full of beautiful
priestesses whose only pleasure in life is curing the
illnesses of passing sailors. I bet they'd do a lovely job on
your foot.'

'Stop the boat!' yelled Philoctetes.

'Sorry, can't,' said Odysseus casually. 'We've got to get
to Troy as soon as possible.'

'Well, you'll just have to get there without me,' said
Philoctetes and, grabbing his silver bow and arrows, he
hobbled across the deck, dived into the water and swam
to the shore.

Odysseus looked happy, and Philoctetes looked
around the island. There was not a priestess in sight. All

he could see were black rocks and white bird droppings.

'Hey, wait a minute!' he yelled.

'Sorry!' Odysseus yelled back from the boat. 'My mistake. Apparently you're on Lemnos, not Limnos. Limnos is somewhere totally different. Look, I tell you what. We'll come and pick you up when we've beaten the Trojans.'

'It shouldn't take long,' shouted Agamemnon. 'They're just a bunch of savages.'

'No!' cried Philoctetes. 'NOOOOOO!'

But it was too late. The boats slowly disappeared over the horizon and he was alone. Tricked by Odysseus. Alone with his rotting foot, and his pain, and no promise of their return.

And so the boats sailed on towards Troy. For days and nights they sailed through calm seas, a calm given to them because of the sacrifice of Agamemnon's daughter. Finally, one morning, as the sun came up in the east, the Greeks spied the great city of Troy – the city they had come to destroy. It shone in the morning light like a jewel dropped in the middle of the large grassy plain which surrounded it. Spires and turrets and minarets sparkled and glowed; they were the colour of birds' eggs, pale pinks and blues and greens.

At first the Greeks sighed in amazement. But then they noticed that the whole city was fringed by a massive, grey wall, thirty metres high and thirty metres thick, without a single gap in it.

It was a beautiful city, one that no man would want to destroy – and with a wall like that, perhaps no man could.

All at once there was a deafening crunch as a thousand boats hit the shore and were heaved up past the high-water mark. Exhausted after their long journey, the men fell on to the sand. They had arrived at last.

There was a long silence.

'What do we do now?' asked Diomedes, scratching a pimple on his nose.

'I'm going to send a messenger telling them to surrender,' said Agamemnon.

'Good idea,' replied Diomedes. 'As long as it's not me. Anyone barmy enough to go in there will come out with a knife in his back.'

'In that case,' said Ajax, 'send Odysseus.'

Odysseus thought about refusing, but everyone agreed that he was the only person who had the cunning to get in and back out again alive – so he didn't bother.

Agamemnon gave his order, 'Odysseus – go to King Priam and tell him we want Helen back. If we can have her, we'll go in peace. If not, we'll burn his city to the ground.'

'Some message,' murmured Diomedes.

'And, by the way, tell him we want a thousand chests of gold to repay us for all the trouble he's caused.'

Oh no, thought Odysseus, wondering which bit of his back the knife would go in.

An hour later, Odysseus found himself staring into old Priam's eyes. 'Why do you want Helen?' Priam was saying. 'She came of her own free will.'

'Free will!' replied Odysseus. 'I heard that your son Paris tied her up, put a bag over her head and carried her off on his shoulder.'

'Is that true?' asked Priam, turning to Helen. But Helen was gazing out of the window at the huge Greek army that was now camped across the plain.

'Sorry – what?' she said, chewing on a toffee. 'I wasn't listening.'

She's got fatter in the face, thought Odysseus.

'No, it's absolutely not true,' interrupted the incredibly bronzed man standing next to her. 'She came here because we are deeply in love with each other.'

Odysseus stared at him. It was Paris. The cause of all the trouble. He had curly, golden hair that came down to his shoulders, and the back of his shirt collar was turned up.

'She's the darlingest, most wonderful girl in the world and I would rather die than give her up.'

'It's not you dying that I'm worried about, Paris,' snapped Odysseus. 'I'm worried about your father dying, about your mother dying, about your brother Hector dying, and about hundreds of innocent men and women in Troy slaughtered for no reason. And I'm worried about me. I don't fancy dying just because you've got a crush on a chubby fifteen-year-old, especially when she's someone else's wife.'

Priam looked at Paris. For a moment, Odysseus thought he might be winning the argument. But then there was a loud laugh from across the room and there stood Hector, the great Trojan hero. He was bare to the waist and incredibly muscly. He was covered all over in tattoos, with a sweat band round his head and a bandolier full of throwing knives across his chest. He laughed long and loud and then ambled over to Odysseus.

'Come on, Odysseus,' he said. 'Your generals don't care about Helen. They want our money and our city and our trade, and above all, they want to fight. No, you go and tell Agamemnon that we won't surrender. If we gave you Helen back today, you'd still find an excuse to wipe us out tomorrow.'

Priam agreed. Paris agreed. Helen had another chocolate. Odysseus knew that this was an argument he wouldn't win.

So it was war.

Hector walked back with Odysseus towards the city gates. He was a proud man and an honest one.

'Come,' he said, 'I'll show you the city you want to burn to the ground.'

And what Odysseus saw made him sad, because Troy was indeed a beautiful city. They walked down a wide street lined with date palms, where crowds of laughing children stood watching a troupe of snake charmers. The street led into the city square, with strange and beautiful fountains spraying gentle mists of water over passers-by, while old people in white hats and coats played a game of bowls.

But then they turned a corner, and before him Odysseus saw something even more strange and beautiful than all the rest.

Completely surrounded by soldiers dressed in blue leather armour with scarlet sashes, was a dome-shaped building. It was white and shiny and completely round, and at its centre was a tiny door.

'It's the church of the White Goddess,' said Hector, as Odysseus stood still, looking on in wonder. 'Enter.'

He walked up to the building, the guards parted and he opened the tiny ivory door. Inside there was flute music. Lights flickered and strange-smelling smoke filled the air. And there in the very centre, on an ivory pedestal, sat a little white figure, a metre high. It was a woman with a fat belly and a grin on her face.

'It's the Goddess,' whispered Hector. 'She protects the city.'

'She winked at me,' said Odysseus.

'No, she's made of stone,' said Hector. 'It must have been a trick of the light.'

'Possibly,' said Odysseus, as he walked away. 'But there's only one way to protect this city, and that's to stop this war.'

'And how can we do that?' asked Hector.

'I've got an idea,' replied Odysseus.

'What?' Even in Troy men knew that when Odysseus had an idea, it was worth listening to.

'A duel. Hand-to-hand single combat. Paris fights Menelaus. Lover against husband. If Paris wins, he keeps Helen and we Greeks promise never to bother Troy again. But if Menelaus wins, we get Helen and the gold. That way, only one person gets killed and the city is saved.'

'It's worth a try,' answered Hector, and as he walked back through the city, past the men, the women, and the children playing, all of them at peace, he dared to smile with hope.

Next morning, the two great armies faced each other.

Out of the Trojan line stepped Paris. He looked so stylish, as he glided forward, with a piece of gold round his neck, one round his wrist, one round his ankle and a helmet in the crook of his arm, forged entirely of gold.

Out of the Greek line stepped Menelaus. He was short and squat and sweaty and hairy. He stared at the young man who'd stolen his wife and his lips curled in contempt.

A horn sounded. Menelaus immediately drew his sword, let out a throaty growl and rushed at Paris.

It wasn't a pretty fight. Menelaus just hacked and hacked at Paris, who backed away and kicked and spat. Then in a moment, they were in close, scratching and clawing and biting each other.

Suddenly, Menelaus brought his knee up hard. Paris jack-knifed and fell to the ground. With a roar of fury, Menelaus grabbed him by his helmet and began to whirl him through the air. Faster and faster he went, his feet and legs flying round and round, and as the strap bit into his neck, Paris turned crimson, then purple, then green, then deathly white.

The Greek army started cheering with delight. They thought it was all over, when suddenly – SNAP – his helmet strap broke and Paris went shooting up into the air. Higher and higher he went, and then down, down,

down, down, he fell, until with a crunch he landed fifty metres behind the Trojan lines.

He groaned, picked himself up, and staggered away from the fight and back into Troy. Not believing their eyes, Priam and Hector rushed after him and found him in Helen's bedroom. His face was buried in her neck and he was sobbing wildly. He knew if he went back out there, he would die.

'Get back out and fight!' yelled Hector.

'Ooooh, hooooh, oooooo,' went Paris.

'I don't think he's at all well,' said Helen, popping a fig in her mouth. 'Can't we send them a sick note?'

Hector and Priam thought for a moment, knowing what it would mean if Paris refused to fight now. A moment later they sprinted back to the front of the Trojan lines.

'A miracle, a miracle!' shouted Priam. 'As my son, Paris, was flying through the air, the White Goddess, disguised as a vulture, swooped down from the sky, picked him up in her beak and flew off with him to her sanctuary on the island of Syphos. We tried to catch him, but we didn't have a chance. She said she'd bring him back in about a fortnight.'

'RUBBISH!' yelled Achilles.

'It's a fix!!!' screamed big Ajax. 'Let's get the lying Trojan scum!' And immediately the whole Greek line charged the Trojans in a wave of fury. The Trojans turned and fled back into the city.

CRASH! The huge gates slammed shut just as the Greeks reached the walls. But that didn't stop them. The Greeks shouted and swore and banged the doors with their fists. And no one shouted and swore louder than Achilles, the Greek hero.

'Get back!' called Agamemnon, sensing danger, and he and Odysseus and Diomedes tried to pull the men away. But they were consumed with fury. They had just seen fair victory snatched out of their fingers, and now they weren't in a mood for walking away. They clawed at

the stones with their bleeding hands, trying to tear the walls down. They wanted to win and go home.

But suddenly their cries of fury turned to screams of pain, as high up on the battlements the Trojans began shooting volleys of arrows and spears down on their attackers. And then screams of pain turned to wails of agony as – WHOOSH! – huge vats of boiling oil came cascading down the walls.

'Retreat! Retreat!' screamed Agamemnon. And retreat they did, carrying their wounded and their dead with them, leaving a trail of blood patterned on the plain behind them.

The war had really begun. Now there was no turning back.

The last to return to camp was Achilles. There were tears in his eyes and a young, blond-haired boy in his arms. 'They don't fight fair,' he yelled. 'Look what they've done to Patroclus. They've burnt his leg – really badly.'

'It's only a scald,' said Odysseus. 'I'll get the doctor to look at it later.'

'No, thank you very much!' snapped Achilles. 'I'll look after him myself, thank you. He is my best friend, you know.' And he carried Patroclus back to his tent.

A difficult man he was, this great fighter.

'We'll never beat the Trojans with a frontal assault,' said Agamemnon, when all the Princes gathered late that night. 'We'll have to starve them out.'

'That'll take years,' answered Odysseus.

'Not if we plan it properly, it won't. I'll put such a ring of soldiers round Troy that nothing can possibly get through. In three months Priam will come out crawling.'

So the siege began, and for two and a half months the ring stood solid. Not an ant got in or out of Troy without being spotted. It looked as though the Greeks would indeed win – even Helen got thin.

But then boredom began to set in. A ship arrived from Greece and half the army broke ranks to see if they'd got any letters. Then a shipment of booze arrived and the whole camp was legless for three days. There were fights, desertions, and every time the ring of troops was broken, Hector's commandos sneaked out into the countryside and brought back food.

So, a whole year went by and the Trojans still hadn't surrendered. Then two years, three, four, five. Occasionally there were skirmishes; sometimes the Trojans sneaked out and murdered a few Greek guards; sometimes the Greeks rode out into the surrounding countryside and pillaged a small town.

Six years went by, then seven, then eight, nine. Boys who had joined up were now young men. Young men were growing older. One oldish soldier grew very old and died. Time, time, time passed, and the long, dull war dragged on.

Until one day, at the beginning of the tenth year, Achilles burst into Odysseus' tent.

'That man!' he stormed. 'I knew he was a fool, but I didn't realise he was a thief.'

'Who?'

'Who do you think? AGAMEMNON!'

'Oh no,' sighed Odysseus wearily. 'What's happened this time?'

'Well,' spat Achilles, 'you know that brilliant attack Patroclus and I worked out?'

'What!' said Odysseus. 'You mean last week, when you set fire to that little village and killed everyone in it?'

'Yes, that's the one,' replied Achilles, proudly. 'And you know the valuable trophies I heroically rescued?'

'The church candlesticks and the black and white cow?'

'Yes,' said Achilles. 'AND the rather attractive slave girl with the turned-up nose.'

'Oh no!' said Odysseus.

'Oh yes!' answered Achilles. 'Agamemnon has stolen them!'

'Let's go and take a look,' said Odysseus. And muttered under his breath, 'Boys, boys.'

Agamemnon's tent was made of gold lamé covered with paintings of little stick men killing each other. Odysseus announced himself and the flap lifted. There was Agamemnon, leader of the Greeks, tucking in his tunic and straightening his hair.

'What's the fuss?' he snapped.

Achilles pushed past Odysseus. 'Where's our slave

girl?' he yelled. Achilles was the greatest fighter in Greece – had been since the day a sword was first placed in his hand – but sometimes he could behave just like a baby.

'What slave girl?' asked Agamemnon innocently. At which moment a head popped out from behind the flap of the tent. It looked very much like a slave girl.

'Her! Her! Her! Her!' screamed Achilles, jumping up and down in fury.

'Oh, that slave girl,' said Agamemnon. 'Well, you see, as your commanding officer, I have to check each item personally and then decide to whom it's allocated.'

'You're a thief!' yelled Achilles.

'No, I'm not!' screamed Agamemnon.

'And a liar!' bellowed Achilles.

'I am NOT a liar!' bawled Agamemnon.

'Yes, you are,' shouted Patroclus over the pair of them.

'You keep out of this,' hissed Agamemnon. But it was too late. By now the whole army was gathered, staring open-mouthed as their two great heroes, leader and fighter, squared up to each other, like children in a play-ground.

'Don't you speak to my friend Patroclus like that!' yelled Achilles.

'I'll speak to him how I like,' sneered Agamemnon. 'I am his commanding officer.'

'You?' spat Achilles, jutting out his face, full of scorn. 'You couldn't command a basket full of kittens. I'm sick

of being commanded by you. Thanks for ten years of nothing. I resign. Here and now, I resign.'

And with that he threw down his sword, threw down his helmet, and stormed back towards his tent.

'So do I,' said Patroclus. 'I resign too.' And he slammed his dagger down on the ground and flounced after Achilles.

At first no one watching could believe it. It was as though a huge oak tree, the tree that was their army, had been split right down the middle.

Within seconds the word had spread round the camp. The army's hero, Achilles, the man who could shatter a rock with his bare hands, wouldn't fight any more and had set up camp on the other side of the beach. A few soldiers, fighters, young men, stomped across the sand to join him straight away. But then more followed, older men, who knew the Greeks couldn't win without Achilles. And then more, even more, until the army was split into two halves, one half on either side of the great beach.

'Do what you like!' yelled Agamemnon. 'I don't need you!!!'

And as he said it, a crash of thunder broke through the heavens, as if someone from up above was laughing. And a vulture flew overhead, with a small, crying animal between its teeth.

'I don't need you, or any of your friends,' Agamemnon hollered again.

But Odysseus just shook his head. 'I think you do, Agamemnon,' he muttered. 'I think you do. Unless Achilles is with us, the walls of Troy will never fall.'

And he looked towards the black and gold tent where Achilles lived, and he was filled with regret that the anger of Achilles had ever begun.

4
Achilles Heel

The Greek army was now hopelessly divided. There were two camps and two leaders.

Agamemnon was furious and took it out on his men. He woke them up at 4 o'clock every morning and made them do exercises: one hundred press-ups, one hundred sit-ups and a five-kilometre run. They became extremely fit but they weren't having much fun.

Meanwhile Achilles' men spent their days surfing and sunbathing. They were less fit but they had incredible tans.

One morning, as usual, Agamemnon's troops were charging at sandbags with their lances while Achilles' army whistled and catcalled and generally indicated that they thought Agamemnon's men were a bunch of idiots.

Suddenly Odysseus stopped and frowned. 'I think I hear something,' he said.

'It's only Patroclus and the rest of Achilles' lads,' replied Diomedes.

But Odysseus shook his head. 'No, it's not that. It's a low rumbling noise – like thunder.'

Diomedes could hear it now. So could the rest of the men. They turned towards Troy – and what they saw filled them with terror.

In the middle of the Trojan plain was a solitary figure on a white horse. He was bared to the waist, covered in tattoos and his sword was pointing straight towards Agamemnon. It was Hector, the Trojan hero. Behind him a huge army rumbled out of the Trojan gates: two thousand horsemen in dark blue leather with scarlet sashes, followed by wave upon wave of foot soldiers with axes and scarlet shields.

'Get back to the tents and fetch your weapons!' yelled Agamemnon. But the Trojans were galloping furiously

across the plain now and the Greeks had no time. They panicked and started to run this way and that in blind terror.

Over in Achilles' camp the men were waiting for their orders. Should they fight? After all it was their fellow Greeks who were under attack. 'Serves them right,' said Achilles. 'Let's go for a swim.'

Meanwhile, in desperation, Odysseus had drummed a few of his least panicky men into line and Diomedes was passing out the lances which he'd yanked from the sandbags. The first wave of Trojan horsemen burst on them. The Greeks hurled their lances and brought the Trojans tumbling to the ground. They grabbed the dead Trojans' swords and turned to face the second wave.

More Greeks were running back to help. Agamemnon had found a huge ball and chain and was whirling it round his head, crushing Trojan skulls like coconuts.

Menelaus had ripped up a tent by its tent pole and was thwacking at the legs of the Trojan horses.

Then big Ajax appeared, waving a sword the size of a small tree and carrying a vast shield. Suddenly from behind it a tiny man popped out, threw a tiny lance and disappeared behind the shield again.

'Who's that?' asked Odysseus.

'He's big Ajax's cousin,' explained Diomedes.

'What's his name?'

'Little Ajax.'

Once more the little man appeared from behind the

shield, then – OOOFF – he let out a gasp of surprise. A Trojan spear was sticking right through him.

'Stretcher bearers!' shouted big Ajax, and two men came ducking and weaving towards him with a leather stretcher.

But – WHOOSH – out of nowhere the leading bearer fell to the ground with an arrow in his eye. It was one thing to fire at soldiers, but someone was deliberately shooting the medical teams.

Fifty metres away, skulking high up a tree and well out of range, was a bowman. He was wearing scarlet eyeshadow and he had dark blue braids plaited in his hair. It was the Trojan prince, Paris. He let fly another arrow and – WHUMPH – the second bearer fell to the ground.

'We can't stay here!' shouted Agamemnon. 'We're sitting ducks. Get down to the beach or they'll burn our ships.'

On and on came the Trojans with Hector in their centre, smiling and relaxed, his sword cutting down any Greek who crossed his path.

Soon the whole of Agamemnon's camp was in flames. Even Agamemnon's gold lamé tent was melting and shrinking like a burnt crisp packet. Step by step the Greeks retreated until they came to the high-water mark where their boats lay beached.

'Drag them down to the shore and cast off!' yelled Agamemnon.

'You're joking,' replied Odysseus. 'That's surrender.'

'Yes, stand and fight!' roared Diomedes.

'All right,' grumbled Agamemnon. 'I was only testing to see how brave you were.'

Back at their camp Achilles' men sat and stared dumbly at the slaughter.

'Aren't you going to fight?' shouted Patroclus suddenly.

'No, I'm not,' said Achilles. 'Do my back, Patroclus,' and he passed him the suntan oil. But Patroclus hurled it to the ground.

'They're our comrades, Achilles. If you don't want to fight, let me wear your armour. The Trojans are scared stiff of you. If they think you're joining the battle they'll lose their nerve and our countrymen will be saved. Let me fight for you. *Please.*'

Achilles looked worried, but then he nodded and smiled.

By now the Greeks had been driven up on to the decks of their ships and Trojan horsemen were riding round and round them firing blazing arrows into the rigging. And if that wasn't bad enough, the Trojan foot soldiers were slinging grappling hooks and rope ladders over the side and trying to climb on board.

The Greek heroes were doing their best. Ajax's boat was blazing and six Trojans raced along the deck towards him. But Ajax grabbed one by the legs, whirled him round his head, and knocked the others down like ninepins.

Poor Diomedes had an arrow through his foot pinning him to the deck. But he was fighting round and round in circles cutting down every Trojan in his path.

And as for Odysseus, he was being chased up the rigging by half-a-dozen axe-wielding maniacs. Higher and higher he climbed until he had nowhere left to climb, just a fifty-metre drop below him. Desperately, he broke off the top of the mast and hurled it at the leading Trojan but the others kept coming. In ten seconds he knew he'd be dead. He thought of Ithaca, he thought of Penelope. He thought what it would be like to have five swords stuck in his chest.

Then suddenly there was a cry of terror and the Trojans froze. On the beaches, in the water, on deck and up the mast there was silence. Why? What had they seen that could make them so terrified at the very moment when they had the Greeks on the run?

Out of the sun, huge and shining like a mirror, a mammoth figure in silver and gold armour appeared.

Then a cry went up – it was the same cry from both sides, but the Greeks screamed with joy, the Trojans with terror.

'It's Achilles! Achilles has joined the battle. Achilles, the greatest fighter in the world. Achilles who can crush an elephant with one hand.'

And the Trojans yelped, 'Let's get out of here!' And they all began to run back towards Troy.

'Stop! Stop!' called Hector. But a dreadful panic had seized his men. Some fell, others trampled over them. Soon the city gates were choked with two thousand soldiers trying to squeeze back into Troy and still the terrifying figure kept coming. Would it kill all of them? Would the war end this very afternoon?'

A dying Trojan lay in the figure's path. He'd never done anything particularly noteworthy in his life. He was a very ordinary soldier, but this was his moment of glory. He reached up and clutched the leg of the huge silver and gold monster. Why he did it no one will ever know. Maybe he was just begging for mercy. But the monster stumbled, fell, its helmet rolled off and a shout went up, 'It's not Achilles, it's Patroclus!'

Suddenly there was a bloodthirsty roar – the most bloodthirsty any man has ever heard – and the last thing Patroclus ever saw was the entire Trojan army bearing down on him and the points of two thousand spears speeding towards his throat.

Back at the beach, the Greeks were putting out the fires and regrouping when they heard the news of the death of Patroclus.

'Go and tell Achilles,' ordered Agamemnon.

'You're the commander,' replied Odysseus. 'It's your job.'

'I'm not going on my own,' said Agamemnon. 'You come with me.'

Achilles was lying on his bed in his dressing gown.

'What do you want?' he asked sulkily.

At first Agamemnon didn't dare to answer.

'Tell him his friend Patroclus is dead,' whispered Odysseus.

'Your friend Patroclus is dead,' said Agamemnon.

'Say you're sorry, it's all your fault,' whispered Odysseus.

'I'm sorry, it's all my fault,' said Agamemnon. 'You can

have the slave girl back if you like.'

But Achilles wasn't listening. His face was drained of blood; it looked like a death mask. Then, letting out a howl like a wolf, he pulled out his huge, golden knife and lifted his hand to cut through his own throat. In a flash Odysseus grabbed his arms and looked deep into his face.

'Revenge,' he hissed. 'You don't want death, you want revenge.'

Achilles' eyes half focused. His mind was in a turmoil. Then, 'Yes,' he said. 'Call the men. There's going to be a massacre.'

'Take it easy,' urged Odysseus. 'Let the men rest first. They haven't even had their breakfast yet.'

Achilles' eyes clouded over.

'Patroclus always used to make a lovely breakfast,' he said. 'He used to cut the toast into little soldiers.' Then he sighed and asked softly, 'Who killed him?'

'The whole Trojan army,' answered Agamemnon.

'And where's his body?'

Odysseus pointed towards the walls of Troy. 'I shouldn't think there's much left of it though,' he said.

In a moment Achilles was up and running across the battlefield. He found Patroclus looking like a hedgehog with two thousand spines, and Hector's sword plunged deep into his heart.

With tears in his eyes Achilles plucked out the spears, picked up the corpse, and carried it back to the beach.

In silence he unbuckled the armour from his dead friend and put it on. For a moment he stood barefoot and helmetless, looking at the body of Patroclus. Then he took a sword and shield . . .

Now you may be interested in this shield because as shields go it was pretty extraordinary. However, if you aren't, this book is not going to try and persuade you. It's perfectly all right if you rush on to the next page.

For those of you who have stayed put, the shield was of solid bronze inlaid with ebony and ivory and had been forged by an extremely grumpy metalsmith called Hephaistos who had bad breath and a limp.

In the centre of the shield was a hideous gorgon's head with adders and cobras writhing in its hair. Its mouth was full of razor sharp teeth which held the wriggling bodies of its victims, and slobber dribbled down its cheeks. This slobber dribbled into a stream which was full of piranha fish who were viciously attacking a donkey which was crossing the stream with a hunchbacked pedlar on its back. The pedlar was making his way towards a little village on the other side of the stream where there was a fête with sideshows and round-abouts and guess-the-weight-of-the-cake competitions and a little band with a fat singer and parties of jolly peasants dancing and drinking huge barrels of wine. Up above, the gorgon's eyes were twinkling with sadistic delight and its huge green hairy claws were bearing down on the village. And looking up at it was a tiny little boy and he was firing a teeny weeny little arrow at the gorgon from a teeny weeny little bow.

'That's some shield,' whispered Odysseus.

'Yes,' said Achilles. 'But it's murder to clean.' Then he slowly walked over to his horse. He was going to fight the Trojans alone.

As he put one bare foot into the stirrup, the horse turned its head and looked at Achilles. 'You know you're going to die, don't you?' it said.

'Pardon?' replied Achilles. As far as he knew his horse had never spoken before, and he didn't think it had chosen a very good time to start.

'Out there on the battlefield,' continued the horse. 'You'll be pushing up daisies tomorrow.'

'Yes, probably,' said Achilles in a rather irritated voice, 'but that's all part of the job, isn't it?' And he kicked the horse into a trot, and galloped towards Troy.

There were small clusters of Trojans dotted all over the battlefield and when he came to them he killed them. Against Achilles no man stood a chance.

A river wound its way across the plain. As he began to cross, a whole platoon of Trojans rose from the banks and attacked him. Waist deep in water he fought them, thrusting and cutting and dragging them under the surface. On and on he spurred his horse. Deeper and deeper they went until horse and rider were completely submerged, but still Achilles went on fighting.

Now he was fighting the river itself. Water and weed and Trojan bodies were all caught up in the whirl of Achilles' fury. There ahead of him were the walls of the city. The gates were barred and every single Trojan had disappeared – every single Trojan, that is, except one. Standing in front of the main gate was Hector.

The two great heroes faced each other. Hector with a handful of throwing spears gently bobbing up and down in his hand and Achilles, bareheaded, barefooted, his eyes blank and unblinking, with his sword held loosely by his side.

Hector threw a spear. Achilles caught it and he snapped it in two. Hector threw another and another, but each one he threw Achilles caught and broke, until he was down to his final spear. Hector looked deep into the eyes of his enemy. And though he knew he was the greatest warrior in Troy and that at this moment Troy depended on him, he realised that now was not the time to fight.

'Open the gates,' he whispered softly to his fellow Trojans. 'I'm coming back in.'

'No, you're not,' said a voice from behind the gates. It was Paris and he was slightly shocked that his brother should dare to suggest such a thing. 'This is your day of glory,' he reminded him.

'No it isn't,' whispered Hector.

'Yes it is.'

'No it isn't. Open the gates.'

'You kill Achilles,' said Paris. 'Then I'll open the gates.'

Once more Hector looked at his enemy. *Should I beg for mercy?* he thought. *Shall I offer him Helen and the thousand chests of gold?* But in Achilles' eyes Hector could see nothing but madness. There was only one course of action for a sensible hero to take at a moment like this. He ran away.

He sprinted as fast as he could round the walls of the city to escape from the barefooted madman who wanted to kill him.

But Trojan heads were popping up all over the battlements; and they were not heads he particularly wanted

to see at a moment like this: his father, his brothers, his cousins, his second cousins, his aunties.

'Stand and fight,' they were screaming. 'Turn round and slaughter him.'

But faster and faster Hector ran, with the sound of Achilles' feet padding in his ears. Until suddenly the sound stopped. Still running, he looked behind him. Achilles was nowhere.

He'd made it. He'd live to fight another day.

THUMP! He'd run into something – a suit of armour, a silver and gold suit of armour, Achilles' armour. Hector drew back his arm to hurl his final spear. Achilles' sword flashed. Hector fell to the ground.

'Kill me,' gasped Hector. 'But let my body be treated with honour.'

Slowly, deliberately, Achilles shook his head. Then the Trojans watched in horror as he hacked their hero into the dust. Achilles tied the body to the saddle, mounted his horse, and slowly rode round Troy with dead Hector dragging in the dust behind him.

The Trojans watched in silent horror. Hector's father felt his heart break. And as for Paris, he beat his fists

against the battlements in frustration. How dare anyone treat his brother like this? Quickly, he ran into the town, heading for the temple of the Goddess. He burst in through the tiny door, and seized the old priestess by the shoulders.

'Poison,' he hissed. 'Fetch me some deadly poison.'

Round and round the walls of Troy rode Achilles until the sun began to set. Then he yanked on his horse's head and rode back towards the Greek camp.

High up on the battlements Paris dipped an arrow into the stinking bowl of green smoking venom and drew his bow. The arrow sped towards its target and VUMP! bit deep into Achilles' heel. But Achilles didn't flinch.

He just kept on riding, dragging Hector's body behind him.

By the time he arrived back at camp it was dusk – a wet misty cold dusk. The whole Greek army watched in silence as he rode up to Agamemnon.

Then he stopped, slowly toppled off his horse, and crashed on to Hector's lifeless body.

Odysseus bent down beside him and lifted up his eyelids. He turned to Agamemnon. 'He's dead,' he said. 'Achilles is dead.'

'I told him that would happen,' grumbled the horse. But no one was listening.

5
The Revenge of the White Goddess

The entire Greek army had been sitting on the wet grass for hours listening to Archbishop Calchas' sermon.

'And now,' droned the Archbishop, 'for the final part of our funeral service.'

Diomedes stifled a yawn and clouted the soldier in front of him, who was playing patience with a pack of cards.

'Our old hero Achilles is dead,' continued Calchas. 'We cannot win the war until we have a new hero.'

General Agamemnon now stepped forward in his best uniform and lifted up the huge suit of silver and gold armour.

'This belonged to my dearest friend, Achilles,' he said with tears in his eyes. 'I now present it to the best and bravest soldier in the Greek army: he shall be our new hero.'

The soldiers stirred. At last the moment had arrived. Who would it be? Which man among them was great enough to take over from Achilles?'

Big Ajax stood up. 'Thank you very much,' he said. 'It's a great honour.'

'Sit down!' shouted Diomedes.

'What do you mean?' answered Ajax. 'I'm the best soldier in the Greek army. I've got sacks full of medals to prove it.'

'Rubbish!' shouted Diomedes.

'Oh, rubbish is it? Who do you think's the best then? Your marvellous friend, Odysseus, I suppose.'

'YES!' roared Odysseus' men.

'NO!' roared Ajax's men, and they began jostling and shoving each other and someone was biting someone else's nose.

'Stop it! Stop it! Stop it!' yelled Agamemnon, wading in and pulling them all apart. 'This is a church service, not a football match. We'll have a vote. All those in favour of Odysseus being our hero, raise your swords.'

A forest of swords rose into the air.

'Rights, swords down. All those in favour of Ajax.'

Another forest of swords appeared.

'Who's the winner then?' asked the Archbishop, unable to disguise the excitement in his voice. 'Is it Ajax or is it Odysseus?'

'It's a draw,' said Agamemnon.

'Well, then, let's ask the Trojans what they think,' called Diomedes. 'After all, the best hero is the one the enemy is most scared of.'

So that evening, Agamemnon and Calchas crept up to the walls of Troy and listened carefully to the guards moving above them on the battlements.

'I don't fancy our chances now Hector's dead,' they

heard a Trojan say.

'No,' replied someone else. 'I certainly wouldn't want to meet that Ajax on a dark night.'

'Ajax? You great nellie! It's Odysseus you want to worry about. He may be little but he's as crafty as a barrelful of monkeys.'

'Yes,' they all agreed. 'If anyone can win the war for the Greeks, it's Odysseus.'

So that night there was a big banquet and Odysseus was presented with the armour. There were long, boring speeches of course, but they were followed by roast ox, swan pie and gallons of wine, and soon the entire army was merry – except for Ajax, who was sitting in the corner. The merrier the army got, the gloomier Ajax became.

Odysseus went over to him and said, 'It's not important. It's a fuss about nothing. The armour's too big for me anyway.'

Ajax turned white. 'To be humiliated is bad enough,' he said. 'But to be humiliated by a smarmy, pint-sized know-it-all like you is more than I can bear. Leave me alone! I'm going to kill myself!'

And he ripped open his shirt, drew his sword, and fell on it. Except his sword bent double under his weight and he collapsed on the floor.

The whole Greek army burst out laughing. 'Leave him alone,' scoffed Diomedes. 'He'll soon get over it.'

'I hope so,' replied Odysseus, and stared hard at the bowed figure of Ajax.

Next morning Odysseus wanted some time to think, so he went for a walk on his own. He sat under a plum tree on a hill overlooking the camp and wondered what sort of hero he would make. What was it his grandfather had told him all those years ago? 'When the going gets tough, get a bit crafty, use a few tricks, tell a few whoppers.'

Deep in thought, Odysseus reached up to pick a plum. His hand touched something strange and cold. He looked up. It was a foot. High in the branches Ajax was hanging by his neck . . .

When Ajax's funeral was over, Calchas came fussing up to Odysseus with a bundle full of weapons. 'Morning, hero,' he said. 'You'll be needing these now, of course. Two holy shields, half a dozen holy spears, two holy axes and a holy ball and chain.'

'I'm not that sort of hero,' replied Odysseus. 'We won't defeat the Trojans with brute strength. We're going to have to use a bit of cunning.'

'What do you mean? What are you going to do?'

'First, I'm going to strengthen our army,' said Odysseus. 'Then I'm going to weaken their army and finally I'll find a way to open the gates of the city.'

'And how are you going to start?' asked Calchas.

'Do you remember Philoctetes, the greatest archer in Greece?'

'Yes,' said Calchas. 'You tricked him and had him marooned on the island of Lemnos ten years ago.'

Odysseus smiled. 'Well, if there's one thing our army needs, it's a really good archer.'

A few days later, Odysseus and Diomedes climbed out of their boat on to a deserted island. They hid behind a big, black rock, spotted with seagulls' droppings, and looked down at the pathetic figure below them.

Dressed in seagull feathers, he was sitting outside a cave sticking silver arrows into a small doll carved out of albatross bones. His hands were shaking and he was ill and weak. It was Philoctetes.

'How are you going to persuade him to come back

83

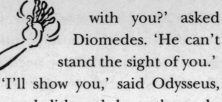

with you?' asked Diomedes. 'He can't stand the sight of you.'

'I'll show you,' said Odysseus, and slithered down the rocks towards the cave.

Philoctetes heard the noise. He looked up at the man coming towards him. Then he looked down at the doll. They both had the same face, man and doll – the face of Odysseus.

Philoctetes let out a howl of anguish, then hurled the doll on to the rocks where it smashed into a thousand pieces.

'Hallo,' said Odysseus. 'Long time no see.'

'What are you doing here?' hissed Philoctetes. 'You've come to kill me.'

'No, I haven't,' replied Odysseus. 'I've come to take you back to Troy.'

Philoctetes was quaking with rage. 'Leave this island,' he ordered. 'I'd rather die than go with you.'

'You sure?' said Odysseus.

'I'm sure,' answered Philoctetes.

'Fair enough,' said Odysseus. 'Still . . . it's a pity about the chest of gold.'

'What chest of gold?'

'Well, Agamemnon was going to give you a chest of

gold for all the trouble you've been caused.'

'I'm not interested,' said Philoctetes, and he limped back into his cave.

'No, of course not,' said Odysseus. 'I respect that. It's a matter of principle, isn't it? Still, it's a shame about the doctor.'

Philoctetes' head popped back out of the cave.

'We've hired this Egyptian doctor, you see, who's a specialist in leg wounds,' persisted Odysseus. 'He'd do a lovely job on your foot.'

'I'm not worried about my foot,' said Philoctetes. 'I've learnt to live with it – learnt to live the life of a wretched creature, an animal – but at least an animal who'll never be tricked again.'

'Yes, I can see that,' agreed Odysseus. 'You've coped really well. I'd better say goodbye then.'

And as he turned to go he said to Diomedes, raising his voice just a little, 'I wonder who they'll make General now?'

'What?'

'Well, it just . . . it's not important really. It's just that they were going to make you a General but, if you're not coming back, I suppose they'll make me one . . . I'm due for a promotion.'

'I'm coming,' said Philoctetes.

'Oh, good,' smiled Odysseus. 'You'll look nice in a General's armour.'

On the voyage back, Philoctetes grew more and more unpleasant. For the first week he did nothing but shovel food into his mouth. For the second he did nothing but talk. He got sleeker, fatter and the old haughty look crept back into his eyes. By the time they got to Troy the sailors wished they'd never gone to get him.

Watching Philoctetes limp down the gangplank, Odysseus put his arm round Calchas' shoulder.

'You'd better get one of your priests to put a mask on and do some mumbo jumbo over his foot . . . and tell him to do it in Egyptian. That should keep our haughty friend quiet for a bit. And tell Agamemnon he's got a new General.'

Calchas nodded. It was a small price to pay for the finest archer in the world.

'I'm off now,' said Odysseus. 'I've got some dressing up to do.'

Sometime later, a filthy beggar hobbled up to the gates of Troy.

'Spare a drachma for a cup of goat's milk,' he whined.

'No begging allowed here,' shouted the guards. 'Get inside, you old filth bag.' And in no time Odysseus was shuffling through the city streets with an enormous moth-eaten hood hiding his face.

Soon he came to Paris' house. At the first-floor window, Helen was stuffing a truffle into her mouth. Odysseus smiled thinly. She'd got a double chin now and little rolls of fat on her wrists.

'Spare a drachma for a flask of sheep's yoghurt,' he called.

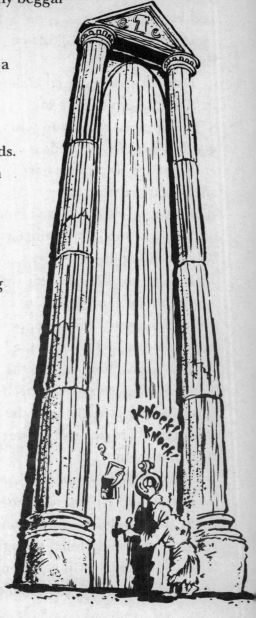

87

'Go away, you horrid beggar,' said Helen.

'It's me – Odysseus,' hissed the beggar.

'Odysseus!' screeched Helen.

'Shhhh. Can I come in?'

Helen raced down the stairs, giggling and frightened.

'What are you doing here?' she asked breathlessly. 'Paris would kill you if he knew.'

'I want to steal the White Goddess,' replied Odysseus. 'Can you help me?'

'I'm not sure if I should,' answered Helen.

'Come on,' urged Odysseus. 'You know you're a Greek at heart.' Helen popped another choc excitedly. Whether she had a heart at all was in doubt.

'You know how much the Goddess means to the Trojans,' Odysseus went on. 'If I can find a way to sneak into the city at night and then get out again with the statue, the Trojans will be terrified. They'll think she's deserted them.'

Helen looked doubtful. 'And remember,' Odysseus added. 'If the Greeks win and you've helped us, it will make things a lot easier for you, won't it?'

'Mmmm,' said Helen thoughtfully. 'I suppose it will. There is a sewer in the garden. Paris says it runs out of the city by the south wall. You could try that.'

'Thanks,' said Odysseus. 'You've been a great help,' and he turned to go.

'Do you fancy staying for a bit?' asked Helen. 'I've got some lovely cream cakes, and Paris won't be home for ages yet.' She smiled, and little dimples appeared just at the top of her plump cheeks.

'Not just now, thanks,' replied Odysseus.

When he arrived back at the Greek camp, the first person to see him was Philoctetes. 'What's this filthy beggar doing here?' demanded the new General. 'Go away, before I set the dogs on you.'

'Don't be ridiculous. You know I'm not a beggar. It's me, Odysseus,' said the beggar.

'How dare you say you're Odysseus,' replied Philoctetes with that sneering look on his face. 'You're wearing filthy rags, you smell like a sewer; you're not a great hero, you're an old tramp. Guards, whip him for his insolence!'

Three burly guards with bullwhips flogged Odysseus until his back was raw, and all the while Philoctetes looked on, his one good eye blazing with triumph. Then, when the whipping was over, he said, 'I do apologise. I seem to have made a mistake. You really are Odysseus, aren't you? Sorry about the 150 lashes.'

'You know what,' said Odysseus, fighting back the pain, 'I really hate you.'

Late that night, when Diomedes had finished bandaging Odysseus' back, the two friends made their way to the place on the south wall which Helen had described. Behind a clump of rushes and rubble, Odysseus could just make out a brown muddy stream. 'It must be the sewer,' he said.

Diomedes' pimply nose twitched in the night air. 'I think you're right,' he sniffed.

They cleared the rubble and behind it found a dark tunnel. Climbing in, they began to inch their way forward. Dark sludge oozed between their feet. Deeper and deeper they went until they were up to their waists in it. Slimy, unseen wriggly things nibbled at their legs and brushed their faces. Rats rustled and chattered in the brickwork. Then, ahead of them, they saw a tiny ring of light and struggled on until they reached a squidgy, rotting manhole. With all his strength, Odysseus heaved it open and they could see the outline of Paris' garden . . . they were inside Troy!

Silently, the two heroes padded down the main street until ahead they could make out the little round church of the Goddess, and stationed round it, the silhouettes of eight Trojan guards.

Odysseus and Diomedes disappeared into the darkness.

THUNK! The first two guards sank to the floor with knives in their backs.

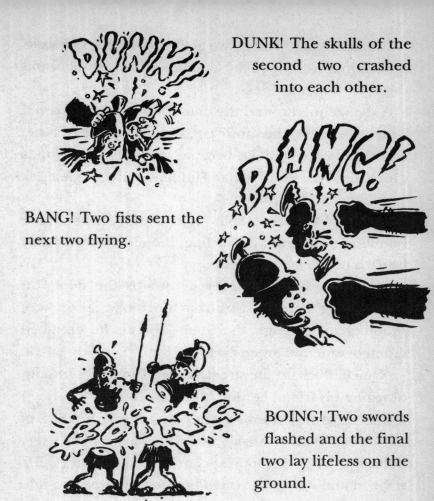

DUNK! The skulls of the second two crashed into each other.

BANG! Two fists sent the next two flying.

BOING! Two swords flashed and the final two lay lifeless on the ground.

Odysseus drew a deep breath, then slowly opened the church door. There were flickering lights and weird music, and through the strange-smelling smoke which drifted round the church Odysseus could make out the ivory pedestal on which the Goddess rested – fat and white and smiling.

Diomedes stayed on guard at the door while Odysseus tiptoed in, gently lifted the Goddess off her pedestal and threw her to Diomedes.

A sigh echoed round the church; the lights flickered faster and faster; the music got louder and out of tune; and the wafts of smoke became great choking clouds which filled the whole room. Suddenly Odysseus felt sick and dizzy and frightened.

CRACK! The roof split in two and bricks came tumbling down from the ceiling. From somewhere they heard a priestess screeching.

Blindly, Odysseus staggered towards the door, his head reeling and pounding from the smoke. Spikes were shooting up through the floor. The air he breathed tasted of emerald-green poison.

'Quick! Back up the street,' called Diomedes huskily, dragging his friend behind him.

But terrifying visions began to appear in front of Odysseus' eyes – snake-headed monsters in every doorway, huge octopuses clutching at his feet. He stabbed and stabbed at them but they disappeared into the darkness.

Then Diomedes heard the heavy tread of soldiers running towards them. He heaved Odysseus back into Paris' garden and pulled him down the sewer. Deeper and deeper they waded, but the soldiers were close behind and gaining. There was torchlight and angry shouts and Diomedes could see the glint of armour.

CHUNG! CHUNG! He hacked away at the old wooden props which held up the crumbling brickwork roof. There was a creaking, a thundering; Diomedes dragged Odysseus forward and WHUUMPH! the whole sewer collapsed in a vast pile of rubble. They could hear the cries and shrieks of terrified soldiers. Then nothing. Silence, except for the rustle of the rats.

'We're nearly there,' said Diomedes and cautiously moved onward.

But behind him Odysseus – white-faced and staring – stood still as a stone. His back was throbbing and his mind was spinning. He was awake, but it was as though he was dreaming. And in this wide-awake nightmare Diomedes was changing shape. He wasn't Diomedes any longer. He was Achilles, pointing his finger at him, accusing Odysseus of having sent him into battle to die.

'You're dead,' mumbled Odysseus. 'Leave me alone.'

But now the figure was transformed into someone else. The ghostly shape of Hector – dead Hector – stood before him.

'I didn't want you to die,' sobbed Odysseus and shook his head and closed his eyes. But when he opened them again, it was Ajax who stood in front of him. Poor stupid Ajax; and he was taking the rope from round his neck and shuffling towards him.

'NO!' cried Odysseus, and thrust his sword at the apparition. 'DIE!' he screamed, but in the middle of his nightmare he couldn't see that his blade was in fact

plunging towards the unprotected back of his best friend. The White Goddess was taking her revenge.

Just in time, Diomedes turned, ducked and SMACK! he belted Odysseus under the chin with the base of the White Goddess, then flung his friend over his shoulders and carried him unconscious to the Greek camp.

Meanwhile, inside Troy, Paris was dragging Helen along the battlements. 'You betrayed me, didn't you!' he shouted. 'You betrayed all of us! Only you knew about that sewer. For ten years my people have been laying down their lives for you and what do you do in return? Conspire with the Greeks to steal our Goddess. Now, once and for all, you must choose whose side you're on. Choose! Them out there, or us in here – which is it to be?' And he pointed out over the no-man's-land between the city and the shore.

Out in no-man's-land, Philoctetes lay waiting. He listened very carefully to where the angry shouts were coming from, then drew his silver bow. THUNK! Helen no longer had to make the choice. Her husband, Paris, lay dead in her arms.

When Odysseus woke up, someone was mopping his forehead. Slowly he opened his eyes. The visions had gone. He was back in his tent, his old friend Diomedes was by his bedside and outside some soldiers were singing a drinking song. Odysseus smiled faintly. 'Now all I need to do,' he whispered, 'is open the gates of the city. Then we'll be back home by Christmas – no problem!'

Somewhere a fox started barking. The last thing Odysseus saw before he fell back into a deep sleep was the White Goddess on the table by his side, and she seemed to be smiling at him . . .

6
Getting In

Odysseus peered out of his tent flap. It was morning. He felt slightly stiff but, given the flogging from Philoctetes and the effect of the temple smoke, he could have felt a lot worse. He stuck two fingers in his mouth and let out a piercing whistle. Immediately a thousand Ithacan soldiers raced out of their tents and gathered round him.

He unrolled a drawing and explained his plan, waving his arms about as he spoke. The soldiers stared at the drawing open-mouthed, then suddenly men were rushing in all directions, fetching drills, saws, hammers, nails and ropes. The big ones dragged huge tree trunks into the camp and the little ones stripped the bark off and sawed them into bits. They built a network of scaffolding and began swarming all over it, shouting instructions, climbing ladders, pulling things up on blocks and tackle.

A whole day came and went. All through the night they worked furiously; hammering, banging and singing popular songs. The other Greek leaders looked on suspiciously. What ever were the Ithacans making?

'Is it a battering ram?' asked Agamemnon.

'No, a battleship,' replied Philoctetes.

'It could be a huge siege tower,' said Menelaus.

The fact is, they had no idea what it was.

Next morning, when the rest of the army woke up, they couldn't believe their eyes. The thing wasn't a weapon of war at all. It was a gigantic children's toy. At the base was an enormous trolley on four huge wooden wheels, on top of that were four great legs, on top of them a vast wooden body, and, sticking up out of the body, a long wooden neck – the whole thing so mammoth it cast a shadow across the entire camp.

'What's it for?' asked Agamemnon suspiciously.

'I'll show you,' replied Odysseus, and he shinned up one of the legs and pulled a lever hidden in the knee. Slowly a secret door in the toy's belly slid open.

'There's room in here for fifty men,' he continued. 'I need forty-nine volunteers to undertake the most daring and heroic mission of the war.'

The whole army stepped forward.

'One place of course will be reserved for me,' said Philoctetes.

'You're a General,' snapped Odysseus. 'You stay here and inspire the troops.'

'I'm a General,' answered Philoctetes. 'So I *order* you to take me.'

'Fine,' said Odysseus, his teeth clenched. 'If that's the way you want it.'

'But what's it supposed to be?' persisted Agamemnon.

'It's not finished yet,' said Odysseus, 'but gather round and I'll tell you my plan.' And it was a plan and a half.

Next morning, up on the Trojan battlements, the guards were yelling and screaming and cheering. What was going on? The whole town joined them on the city walls and looked across the plain towards the sea. They couldn't believe their eyes. The Greeks had gone.

For ten years they'd been camped round the city. For ten years no one could get in or out, and now all that was left of the Greek camp was a few smouldering bonfires and mounds and mounds of rubbish; and far away on the horizon they could make out the distant masts of the Greek ships sailing back home. They'd gone, they'd really gone!

The Trojans began flooding out on to the plain. There was cheering and singing and dancing until a young girl called out breathlessly, 'Look what I've found on the beach!'

Everyone raced towards the shore. Boys, girls, old men, young women, Priam, the Prime Minister and the members of her cabinet. Then they stopped. Down by the sea there was something strange and wonderful. It was huge and white and covered in little magic symbols – bulls' heads, stars, double-headed axes. It was a horse one hundred metres high, with a mane and tail of blue and scarlet feathers; and sitting on top of it on a blue and scarlet saddle was the statue of the White Goddess.

There was absolute silence. Then the whole town tiptoed towards it. Suddenly, 'Duck!' yelled a commando. They all fell flat on their faces.

'There's a movement over there,' growled the commando. Cautiously everyone lifted their heads. From behind a sand dune a little stick was poking and on top of it was tied a grubby white flag.

'Come out with your hands up,' bellowed the commando, and out crept a scruffy, skinny, unshaven Greek soldier with a weaselly face.

'Don't hurt me, please don't hurt me, please, please, please don't hurt me,' he whined as he shuffled towards them.

When he reached King Priam he dropped to his knees. Priam looked at him distastefully and asked, 'Who are you?'

'I'm Private Thersites.'

'And why are you here?'

'Well, sir,' replied Thersites, 'there's been an almighty bust-up in the Greek camp, sir, and Odysseus has been deprived of his Kingdom, sir, and I've run away, sir.'

'What's your story, man?'

'This is my story,' said Thersites, and the whole town sat down to listen.

'It's ten years since we came to Troy, sir, and we weren't winning, but we weren't losing either. And then the boils started. Huge, great, pussy boils all over our bodies, and blackheads, sir, the size of your fist, sir. And

I said to Odysseus, I said, it's all your doing, I said. The White Goddess is angry with us because you stole her statue, I said. But Odysseus said, shut up, Thersites, you don't know what you're on about, he said. So I went to the Archbishop, sir, and I told him Odysseus had stolen the Goddess, and he was livid, sir. And he said we had to give it back and sail for home immediately. And if we didn't we'd be completely cursed and we'd get leprosy and our arms and legs would drop off, sir. And not only that, sir, but we had to give the Goddess a huge present, sir. A present so wonderful she'd forgive us and not drown us on our way home, sir. And Odysseus is in disgrace now, sir, and so he said he'd cut my tongue out, sir. Because I told on him, sir. So I ran away, sir. And here I am, sir, and this is the present . . . this white horse, sir.'

'I have never,' said the Prime Minister, 'heard anything so unconvincing in my entire life.' And she snatched a spear from the nearest soldier and strode round the horse banging on its legs.

'Sounds hollow to me,' she said. 'There must be something inside it.' And she hurled the spear deep into the horse's belly.

Inside the horse a Greek soldier stifled a yawn. This was the most boring job he'd ever undertaken. He'd been keeping still for hours now.

Suddenly, ZONK! the spear passed straight through his legs. He bit deep into his arm to stop himself screaming. Odysseus carefully freed the soldier from the spear and cleaned its point with his shirt.

Outside the horse, the Trojans made a human pyramid. A commando climbed to the top and yanked out the spear. Priam examined it keenly.

'It's quite clean,' he said. 'There's nothing inside the horse. As usual the Prime Minister has got it completely wrong. Guards, fetch some ropes. We'll place the horse in the city square, then everyone will remember the day the cowardly Greeks sailed home.'

'You fool!' screamed the Prime Minister. 'Don't take the horse into the city! Can't you see it's a trick!' The guards stopped. There was doubt in their eyes.

'I'll tell you who's behind this!' she yelled. 'It's, it's . . .' Then something happened that was so extraordinary that the Trojans remembered it for the rest of their short lives.

A huge sea snake rose out of the water and wrapped itself round the Prime Minister's legs. Higher and higher it snaked,

looping itself round her, and then slowly it began to squeeze the life from her body, until her eyes popped, her face turned purple, there was the sound of crunching bones and she fell lifeless on to the sand.

Immediately Thersites jumped up beneath the horse's belly. 'That was a warning!' he cried. 'She tried to stop the horse entering the city and the Goddess punished her.'

'Well said,' agreed Priam. 'Trojans! Get the horse moving and we'll welcome the Goddess back into our city.'

The whole town heaved on the ropes, while the children ran between the horse's legs and threw garlands of flowers in its path. The grown-ups kissed each other and cried and sang hymns. And slowly the great procession crossed the flat, grassy plain back to Troy, with the horse casting its giant shadow over them.

But when they arrived at the city the singing and dancing petered out and everyone stopped and scratched their heads. They had a problem. The horse was too big. They'd never get it through the gates.

'Tear down the wall,' ordered Priam. And hordes of Trojans with sledge-hammers swarmed all over it and began hacking away at the huge stone blocks. Soon the wall was breached, the rubble was cleared and the horse lumbered through the great gaping hole.

Through the town it rolled, its head level with the roof-tops of the tallest houses, until it came to a halt in the city square in front of the church of the Goddess. There was loud cheering and immediately the singing and dancing started up again.

'Wait!' ordered Priam and once more there was silence. 'We can't leave our city wall in this state. For ten years it's been our only protection against sure disaster.'

So the Trojans rushed to their houses and dragged out their old beds and doors and cardboard boxes and crammed them into the hole in the wall until it was completely blocked with Trojan junk.

Then Priam ordered sixty of his finest soldiers to stand guard, pulled the huge metal bolts across the city gates, padlocked them, and put the key round his neck. 'Now we are safe again,' he said. 'Let the celebrations begin!'

There were fireworks, street parties, hundreds of bands, free food and free booze. The Trojans hadn't partied like this since the war had begun. By 3 o'clock in the morning, everyone had crawled exhausted to their beds except for a few drunken revellers who'd passed out in the city square.

The horse stood still and silent. Nothing stirred.

Then there were footsteps. It was Helen with her new Trojan boyfriend. He had permed blond hair, chunky jewellery and his shirt was unbuttoned to the waist.

Helen patted the horse's leg. 'Suppose this is all a trick,' she whispered. 'Suppose the horse is full of Greek soldiers.'

'Oh, come on,' laughed the boyfriend. 'Don't be ridiculous.'

'I'm not. It could be one of Odysseus' little plans. He's so crafty he makes me want to spit.' And she called out, 'Odysseus, are you in there? This is your wife, Penelope. Can you hear me?'

Odysseus sat bolt upright. Penelope had been Helen's best friend, and she was imitating her perfectly.

'How are you?' continued Helen. 'It's ten long years since I've seen you. Come out and say hallo.'

Odysseus began to get up. Was he hearing things? Had Penelope, whom he'd missed so much for ten long years, somehow turned up in Troy?

'It's a trick,' hissed Diomedes. 'A stupid trick. Take no notice.'

'Come out and look at Telemachus, your son,' called Helen. 'He's a big boy now. He's nearly eleven.'

Odysseus started to cry out. But Diomedes slapped his hand over his mouth and forced him back down on to his seat. Slowly, a tear trickled down Odysseus' face.

Outside, Helen's boyfriend was bored. 'Don't be silly, darling. There's no one there. Come on home and let's boogie the night away.' And they left the square with their arms wrapped round each other.

Then, when their echoing footsteps had died away, one of the unconscious revellers got to his feet and tiptoed over to the horse. Only it wasn't a reveller at all. It was Thersites. He shinned up the horse's leg and pulled the lever on its knee. Silently the trap door opened.

'OK, lads?' he whispered.

'OK,' came the reply. And Thersites disappeared again.

'Line up behind me,' ordered Odysseus.

'I'll go first,' said Philoctetes.

'It's my expedition,' replied Odysseus.

'You! You're just a cheap adventurer looking for glory,' jeered Philoctetes. 'I'm the General. I'll go first.'

'Go on then,' said Odysseus.

Philoctetes smiled a crooked smile of triumph and leapt out of the trap door. But he must have wished he hadn't.

There was a sickening thud, then silence. The men

peered down through the darkness
and saw Philoctetes' broken body
dead on the ground.

'There's no ladder,' said Odysseus.
'Why didn't sombody tell him?
War's a terrible thing, isn't it?'

Soon Thersites was back with a
ladder and silently the men
slipped down it. Swiftly they
padded through the shadows.
When they were all in position,
Odysseus gave a hoot like an owl.
From all around the wall there
were muffled grunts and the sound
of Trojan sentries falling to the
ground as the Greeks silently
overpowered them from behind.
Soon it was over. Stage one of the
operation was complete.

Half of them slipped into
Trojan guards' uniforms
and stayed by the gates while
the other half climbed over
the wall, crept down to the
beach and set fire to the huge
mounds of rubbish.

Agamemnon's ships were
hiding just outside the bay.

When they saw the beacons, they rowed quickly and quietly to the beach and wave upon wave of Greek soldiers poured off the ships and sped eagerly towards the city – the city they had never entered.

And then stage two began. The Greeks at the gate quickly pulled down the beds and doors and boxes and yanked them out of the way, so by the time the army reached the wall there was nothing to bar their entry. The gates remained locked, but the soldiers flooded through the hole in the wall, their eyes flashing with blood-lust.

Now it was time for stage three.

As Agamemnon raced into the city, Odysseus stopped him and said, 'You will make sure our men don't harm the women and children, won't you?'

'Have you gone soft or something?' replied Agamemnon.

Odysseus looked on in sorrow, while in the next half hour the most beautiful city in the world was smashed to pieces. Bodies were thrown from the rooftops, beautiful towers and minarets came crashing to the ground, and the Greek soldiers hacked their way through Troy, their arms full of loot, their swords covered in blood.

Menelaus was dripping with sweat from head to foot as he came pounding up to Odysseus, yelling over the deafening noise of slaughter and destruction, 'Where's Helen? Have you seen her?'

Odysseus hadn't, but he knew where to find her.

When they arrived at her house they found it locked. Menelaus hurled himself against the door in animal fury. CRUNCH! It shattered under his weight and he sailed right through it, leaving a Menelaus-shaped hole behind him.

'Guard the door!' he shouted, and Odysseus stood there with his sword in his hand while Menelaus pounded up the stairs.

Odysseus heard the crash of glass as the boyfriend went flying through the window, then the sound of two voices screaming at each other – a man and a woman. Then silence. *Has he killed her?* wondered Odysseus.

No, he hadn't. Helen and Menelaus appeared at the top of the stairs, gazing into each other's eyes.

'You poor darling,' said Menelaus. 'It must have been hell for you. It's all right now, it's all over. I'll take you home.'

Helen smiled at him, then popped a chocolate truffle into her mouth. Her double chins wobbled up and down as she chewed it.

'Is this the face that launched a thousand ships?' Odysseus murmured to himself.

Next morning he stood alone on the sand dunes staring at Troy, just as he had on the morning he had first landed.

But now the city was in ruins, the Greek army was streaming out of the gates carrying great piles of jewels and golden plates, and in the shadow of the city walls a shivering line of Trojan women and children with irons on their hands and feet were waiting to be branded as slaves.

Had it been worth it? Is this what the Greeks had wanted – a beautiful city looted and destroyed, and its people killed or enslaved? Odysseus turned away from the holocaust in sorrow. What had it all been for? He simply had no idea.

Slowly he walked down to the ships, where he congratulated Menelaus on the return of his beautiful wife and hugged his old friend Diomedes goodbye. General Agamemnon shook his hand. Then Odysseus gazed for one last time at the blitzed city. It would never rise again. But somewhere deep in its ashes the White Goddess lay still. Silent and smiling.

Then the boats weighed anchor and Odysseus and the men of Ithaca sailed towards the sunset.

They were going home.